LIFE WITH
CEREBRAL PALSY

BY JEANNE MARIE FORD

Published by The Child's World®
1980 Lookout Drive • Mankato, MN 56003-1705
800-599-READ • www.childsworld.com

Content Consultant: Mary E. Gannotti, P.T., PhD, Department of Rehabilitation
Sciences, University of Hartford

Photographs ©: Jaren Jai Wicklund/Shutterstock Images, cover, 1, 20; Shutterstock
Images, 5, 6; iStockphoto, 8, 10, 16; Olesia Bilkei/Shutterstock Images, 12; Martin
Bowra/Shutterstock Images, 14; Pavel L. Photo and Video/Shutterstock Images, 18

ISBN 9781503825086
LCCN 2017959702

Printed in the United States of America
PA02375

TABLE OF
CONTENTS

FAST FACTS 4

Chapter 1
SOPHIE 7

Chapter 2
NIKKI 13

Chapter 3
ANTHONY 19

Think About It 21
Glossary 22
To Learn More 23
Selected Bibliography 23
Index 24
About the Author 24

FAST FACTS

- Cerebral palsy (CP) is the most common movement disorder in children. It is caused by damage to parts of the brain that control the body's muscles. This damage usually happens before, during, or shortly after birth.

- Some people with CP have very mild symptoms. Others might have trouble with muscles that control walking and **gait**, hand movements, or speech.

- Some people with CP experience **seizures**. They may also have **intellectual** disabilities or problems with hearing and vision.

- There are four main types of CP. Spastic CP is the most common. It causes stiff muscles that are difficult to move. Dyskinetic CP involves too many movements, which may be hard to control. Ataxic CP, the rarest type, causes balance problems and poor **coordination**. Some people have mixed CP. This means they have features of more than one type.

- CP cannot be cured. Some treatments include physical, speech, and **occupational therapy**; medicine; and surgery.

CEREBRAL PALSY EFFECTS ON THE BODY

Cerebral palsy can affect the body in different ways. Either the legs will be affected more than the arms, only one side of the body will be affected (both arm and leg), or the entire body will be affected.

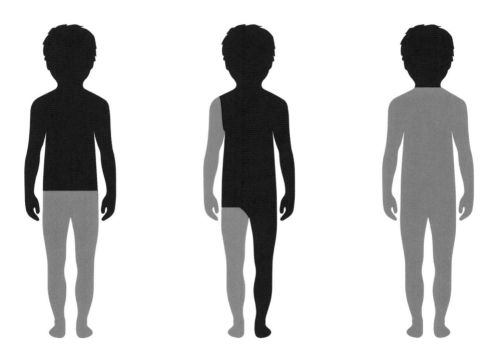

Chapter 1

SOPHIE

Sophie carefully balanced her library book on her walker. She was stuck. She could try to climb the curb in front of her. Or she could walk all the way across the sidewalk to the ramp.

Most nine-year-olds wouldn't have to think about which path to choose. But Sophie did. She had cerebral palsy. Climbing a 6-inch (15 cm) curb was as difficult as scaling a mountain. Walking a few extra steps to the library book drop took as much work as it did for most people to run a long distance.

From behind, Sophie's mom lifted her and the walker from the parking lot onto the curb. Sophie's sneakers scraped the sidewalk as her mom set her down gently.

◄ CP can be detected in a newborn, but it gets easier to diagnose as a baby's brain becomes developed.

They both panted from the effort. Their breath froze in white puffs in the air.

Sophie hated needing help. She worried. How could she be a librarian someday if she couldn't even get herself inside the building?

Sophie spent hours every week doing physical therapy exercises. She walked on a treadmill in a body harness until sweat dripped from her face. Often, her body hurt all over. Sometimes she got mad at her legs. Sometimes she wished she didn't have leg braces. She would love to wear pretty shoes like other girls.

That spring, Sophie went to the hospital for shots to help her leg muscles relax. Then doctors operated on her hips to make them straighter. The surgery would make it easier for her to get around, though she would still use a walker. For weeks afterward, she couldn't stand. She couldn't go to school. She couldn't even play outside.

◀ **Ten percent of children with CP need an aid, such as a walker or braces, to help them walk. Thirty percent of children with CP use a wheelchair.**

▲ **One in four people with CP cannot talk.**

Sophie had a lot of time to think. All of that thinking gave Sophie a great idea. Maybe she could build a walker that she could push over a curb.

She worked with her sister on a design. She borrowed parts from her brother's skateboard. She used big wheels from her dad's lawnmower. After many tries and many failures, her invention was a success! She decided to enter the walker in her school's science fair.

Sophie knew she might not win a trophy for playing sports. But she did win a trophy for her science fair project. That was exciting. What was more exciting was that a curb would never stand in her way again.

ASSISTIVE DEVICES

Many tools called **assistive devices** help people with CP become more independent. Crutches, canes, and leg braces give extra support for walking. Wheelchairs come in many different sizes and types. Many kids who can't walk can ride **adapted** bikes. Special tools can make writing and eating easier. Shoes are made without laces for people who can't tie them. Remote controls can turn on lights or open doors.

Chapter 2

NIKKI

Muscle **spasms** jolted Nikki awake. It was dark outside. Nikki couldn't fall back asleep after that. She counted the minutes until morning.

Her dad finally poked his head into her room. "Good morning, love," he said. He lifted her into her wheelchair and pushed her toward the bathroom. She preferred to zoom around in her power chair. That wasn't safe in this narrow hall. Her steering was not the best.

Nikki's tight muscles drew her hands into closed fists. Her dad squeezed toothpaste onto a toothbrush. He cleaned her teeth one by one. It tickled. She laughed. Then Nikki's dad pulled on her socks. He drew her hair into a neat ponytail.

◀ Some symptoms of CP can change as a child gets older, but overall, the condition does not worsen over time.

▲ Many people with CP are cared for by their family or hired staff, such as nurses.

Nikki's mom fed her some toast. Nikki chewed very carefully so she wouldn't choke. Nikki had trouble controlling the muscles around her mouth. Sometimes she drooled. Nikki couldn't say very many words.

When strangers saw her, they often thought she wasn't intelligent. They were wrong.

Nikki used a device to help her communicate. It attached to the bottom of her wheelchair. She used her big toe to select words and phrases. It could take minutes to say a long sentence. The computer sounded like a robot. Sometimes Nikki dreamed about what her own voice would sound like.

COMMUNICATION

There are many ways that people who cannot speak can communicate. Some methods are simple, such as picture cards or letter boards. Some people use computer technology. Therapists choose communication devices to fit the needs of each person. People who can't use their hands or feet may use pointers attached to their heads to work talking machines. The newest devices work by detecting eye movement.

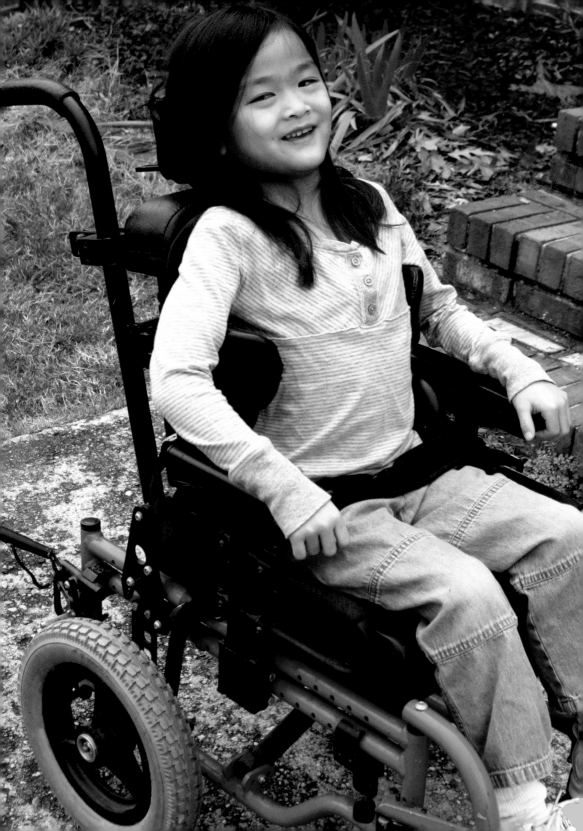

Nikki loved learning. After school, she did her homework on the floor. Her big toe hovered over the tiny keys on her calculator and laptop. Her legs ached by the time she was finished. It once took her six hours to take an English test. A huge blister formed on her big toe.

Sometimes Nikki got frustrated about all the things she couldn't do. She found it much better to think about all the things she could do. It had taken her a long time to learn to chew. Now she could eat anything she wanted. She could play a game of Uno by tapping the cards with her toe. She could laugh with her friends. Nikki looked forward to going to college and getting a job. She dreamt of everything her future might hold.

◄ **World Cerebral Palsy day is on October 6. This day brings awareness to the condition.**

Chapter 3

ANTHONY

The water was the place where Anthony felt most comfortable. It took pressure off his tense muscles. He could float like anyone else. His CP became invisible. Anthony's love of the water began when he was three years old. His mother had taken him to a splash park. He stared at the blue water. The waves lapped gently at the sides of the pool. He slid closer to watch other kids swim and play.

His mom thought Anthony couldn't move from his chair. She turned away to put on sunscreen. When she looked back, Anthony wasn't where she'd left him. He had scooted his way into the pool.

◄ **Physical therapy helps people with CP learn how to move their muscles in different ways.**

▲ **Water therapy has proven to be beneficial for people with CP.**

Anthony began swimming as part of his physical therapy. As he grew older, he wanted to race. His upper body was strong, but his kick was weak. His coaches figured out which strokes worked best for him.

Coaches made special workouts for Anthony. He refused to do them. He wanted to complete the same workouts as the rest of the team. He had learned in physical therapy to work hard. He pushed himself just as hard in swimming.

Anthony's teammates wheeled him to the poolside for every meet. They lifted him out of his chair. As soon as Anthony was in the water, he took off with everyone else. His goal was just to keep up. Usually he did. Sometimes he even won.

Anthony's race times continued to improve. He earned a swimming scholarship for college. He went on to win a spot on the U.S. Paralympic Swim Team. Anthony loved setting records and winning medals. Most of all, he loved the feeling of accomplishment and freedom that swimming gave him.

THINK ABOUT IT

- How could having CP affect a person's relationships with others?
- What types of afterschool activities could kids with CP participate in?
- How could gym class be made more accessible for kids with CP?

GLOSSARY

adapted (uh-DAPT-ed): Adapted means changed to be useful in a new situation. Bikes can be adapted so that people with disabilities are able to go biking.

assistive devices (uh-SISS-tiv deh-VICE-es): Assistive devices are tools made to help people do things that would be difficult without them. Braces and crutches are two types of assistive devices.

coordination (koh-or-duh-NAY-shuhn): Coordination means using different parts of the body together. Ataxic CP causes problems with a person's coordination.

gait (GATE): Gait refers to the way a person walks. Cerebral palsy usually makes a person's gait less smooth.

intellectual (in-tuh-LEK-choo-uhl): Something that is intellectual relates to a person's ability to think and reason. Some people with cerebral palsy have intellectual disabilities.

occupational therapy (ok-yuh-PAY-shuh-null THAYR-uh-pee): Occupational therapy helps people perform tasks they do every day. Occupational therapy might be used to help a person learn to use utensils or write.

seizures (SEE-zhurz): Seizures are sudden attacks that happen when electrical signals go out of control in a person's brain. Some people with cerebral palsy experience seizures.

spasms (SPAZ-uhmz): Spasms are painful muscle twitches. Muscle spasms can make it difficult for people with cerebral palsy to sleep soundly.

TO LEARN MORE

Books

Abdullah, Shaila, and Aanyah Abdullah. *My Friend Suhana*. Ann Arbor, MI: Loving Healing Press, 2014.

Philip, Aaron. *This Kid Can Fly: It's About Ability (Not Disability)*. New York, NY: Balzer & Bray, 2016.

Springer, Mary Beth. *I Have Cerebral Palsy*. Cambridge, MA: Star Bright Books, 2016.

Web Sites

Visit our Web site for links about cerebral palsy:
childsworld.com/links

Note to Parents, Teachers, and Librarians: We routinely verify our Web links to make sure they are safe and active sites. So encourage your readers to check them out!

SELECTED BIBLIOGRAPHY

Andrews, Caitlin. "Weare Sisters Revel in the Spotlight after Inventing Tri-Wheeled Walker." *Concord Monitor*. Concord Monitor, 30 Dec. 2016. Web. 4 Dec. 2017.

"Cerebral Palsy (CP)." *Centers for Disease Control and Prevention*. U.S. Department of Health and Human Services, 13 July 2015. Web. 4 Dec. 2017.

Lee, Steve. "Cerebral Palsy Doesn't Stop Zephyrhills High Swimmer." *Tampa Bay Times*. Tampa Bay Times, 24 Sept. 2014. Web. 4 Dec. 2017.

"Mackenzie's Voice: Living with Cerebral Palsy." *YouTube*. YouTube, 15 Aug. 2016. Web. 4 Dec. 2017.

INDEX

brain, 4

computer, 15

hospital, 9

leg braces, 9, 11

muscles, 4, 9, 13, 14, 19

physical therapy, 4, 9, 20

walker, 7, 9, 10–11

wheelchair, 11, 13, 15

ABOUT THE AUTHOR

Jeanne Marie Ford is an Emmy-winning TV scriptwriter and holds an MFA in Writing for Children from Vermont College. She has written numerous children's books and articles and also teaches college English. She lives in Maryland with her husband and two children.